WILLIAM, THE WHAT-IF WONDER
& HIS SLEEPOVER WORRIES

Written by Carol Wulff, LSW

Contributions by Margaret R. Mauzé, PhD, ABPP
Board Certified Pediatric Psychologist

Illustrations by Clare Willett

IT'S A WONDER PUBLISHING, LLC

Cover and Interior Book Design by
Alex Lucas at Oh The Raven Studio
www.ohtheraven.com

Cover and Interior Book Illustrations by
Clare Willett

DISCLAIMERS:
The author does not intend for this book to be a substitute for medical advice of physicians. The reader should regularly consult a physician in matters relating to their health and particularly with respect to any symptoms that may require diagnosis or medical attention.

Names and persons in this book are entirely fictional. They bear no resemblance to anyone living or deceased.

ISBN 978-1-7349430-0-9

IT'S A WONDER PUBLISHING, LLC

It's A Wonder Publishing, LLC
PO Box 99
Bath, OH 44210-9800

To the brave individuals who have publicly shared
their journey with anxiety so that others know they
are not alone.

-CAROL

To the children, adolescents, and parents who
have allowed me to be part of their journeys.
Thank you for your trust in me.
I am humbled by you all.

And to my three biggest cheerleaders, thank you.

-MARA

To all the people who saw past my what-ifs and saw
the wonder I could do.

-CLARE

Hello, I'm William, as you can see.
A sleepover could be so hard for me.

I'm nervous and scared about being away,
as my what-if worries may get in my way.

They cause me to see what might not be true.

But I have the power to see a new view.

What if I forget the things that I'll use?

Jammies, my teddy, my favorite blue shoes?

What if their house is different than mine?

Don't compare, just have a good time!

What if I can't find the bathroom at all?

William, look! There is a light in the hall.

What if a noise makes my heart start to pound?

The simplest of things can make a strange sound.

What if I miss my mom or my dad?

Join in the fun so you won't be sad!

What if I can't fall asleep late at night?

A book or headphones might make it all right.

What if my family forgets that I'm there?

Your parents and family are very aware!

What if it feels like the night is so long?

You'll be home soon, breathe deep to be strong.

What if I'm nervous but still having fun?

Think good thoughts till the day is done!

I'm the What-If Wonder, what a great night.

I pushed all those what-ifs clear out of sight!

NOTE TO PARENTS & CAREGIVERS

Margaret R. Mauzé, PhD, ABPP

Anxiety is not easy for children or for parents. If you are the parent or caregiver of a child with anxiety, you know how it feels when your child has a barrage of questions and concerns about new experiences. You also know the challenge of encouraging your child to embrace new experiences while helping them develop the skills to make these experiences fun instead of frightening. Children with anxiety can feel an endless flood of worry they find hard to control. For many, this anxiety grows when facing a new experience or environment. Worry impacts children physically, and can cause them to feel short of breath, get stomachaches or butterflies, or have trouble sleeping. It can also impact their thinking, focusing them on all the things that could go wrong or problems that could arise. This often hinders children from considering all the positive things about the experience.

The ability to manage these reactions is largely a learned skill, and parents and caregivers play a crucial role in teaching and showing children ways to manage their anxiety, as well as helping them to put these skills into action. This job can be frustrating, as parents and caregivers may feel ill-equipped to teach their children these strategies, particularly if they also struggle with anxiety or become frustrated when trying to help.

William, the What-If Wonder and His Sleepover Worries is designed to help both parents and children combat the anxious thoughts that children can find so hard to control. Based primarily on the principles of problem-solving and cognitive reframing (i.e., changing the way you think about something), the story verbalizes worrisome "what if" thoughts as well as more positive counter-thoughts. These counter-thoughts are designed to help William find other solutions to his concerns and to remind him of skills he can use to calm his physical reactions. This helps children begin to take control over their anxious thoughts.

When you read this book with your child, you can enhance its benefits in a variety of ways:

• Read the book aloud, taking your time. The rhyming may help younger children commit the principles to memory and make enjoyable reading for children and parents alike.

• Validate William's anxious thoughts while also normalizing his concerns. "It can be hard to sleep away from home. A lot of kids probably feel the way William does the first time they sleep somewhere else." This helps your child feel understood and helps them realize that these feelings of anxiety impact others too.

• Emphasize the solutions provided. "William was concerned he might forget some of his favorite things, but look, his mom helped him make a list to make sure he had everything."

• Ask your child if they have ever felt the way William has, and help them think of more solutions. "William was concerned that he wouldn't find the bathroom. What would you do if you weren't sure where the bathroom was? Who could you ask?"

• Reference the specific things William does to calm his body and mind when he feels anxious, and relate them to your own lives. "Breathe deep to be strong. Sometimes when I'm worried about something, I take ten slow, deep breaths until I feel calmer. What do you do to calm your butterflies down?" Or: "William thinks good thoughts when he is nervous. When I was nervous about my big meeting at work last week, I just kept telling myself that I was prepared and would do my best. What do you tell yourself when you feel nervous?"

• Help your child develop a plan for situations where they might be nervous. For example, if your child is going to stay with their grandparents or going to a new friend's house to play, talk through possible solutions to problems before your child goes. "If Mrs. Jones serves a snack you don't like, what could you do?" "If Grandma forgets to leave the hall light on, how could you fix that? What could you do?" Having a plan can help your child feel prepared for unfamiliar situations and gain confidence in their ability to manage the unexpected.

Using these techniques can help your child to view their anxiety as a separate characteristic. This can help your child feel more control over their worries by learning to address them as a unique part of who they are. For example, a child may want to create their own superhero persona who uses their coping skills to fight back against anxiety. Alternatively, a child may want to practice talking back to their anxiety to feel more control over their feelings. Encourage your child to use their imagination and these skills to feel more control over their anxiety.

If you feel that your child has anxiety that seems out of proportion to the situation, or if your child's anxiety is significantly interfering with their life (preventing them from attending activities they would enjoy, impacting school attendance, disrupting social relationships), please consult with your pediatrician or with a therapist who can work with you and your child on finding more techniques to help manage the anxiety. And if you as a parent feel ill-equipped to help your child with their anxiety, please consider also working with a therapist to learn techniques to help support your child and manage your own concerns.

FOUR SIMPLE STEPS TO PROBLEM - SOLVING

1. Understand the Problem
Have your child verbalize the problem. If your child has trouble identifying the problem, encourage them to identify how their body feels physically.

2. Create a Plan
Generate possible solutions to the problem and decide which one to try. For a child who can identify their physical symptoms only, solutions may focus more on taking deep breaths or counting backwards to help them calm physically.

3. Implement the Plan
Try the solution.

4. Assess the Solution
Check back with your child. Did the plan work? If so, **CELEBRATE.** If not, what could have helped bring a better outcome?

BIOGRAPHY

Carol Wulff, LSW, is a Licensed Social Worker and mother of a child with anxiety. Remembering how painful it was to witness her child's mind racing just to get through the simplest of tasks, she vowed to one day write a book to help others learn how to tackle those annoying what-if thoughts. Cognitive reframing—seeing the same situation in a new way—empowered her child to manage the anxiety and approach new situations with confidence. She created the William, the What-If Wonder book series to help children learn how to use their power to change their view and see past their worrisome thoughts. Carol lives in Medina, Ohio, with her husband and three children.

Margaret R. Mauzé, PhD, ABPP, is a board certified pediatric psychologist. She earned her PhD in clinical child and adolescent psychology from the University of Kansas in 2005. She achieved specialty board certification from the American Board of Professional Psychology in the area of clinical child and adolescent psychology in 2008. She worked at Cleveland Clinic Children's Hospital for seven years before moving into private practice. She has special interest in working with children with acute and chronic medical illness and children struggling with anxiety and depression. She currently lives in San Antonio, Texas, with her husband and two children.

Clare Willett enjoys creating characters and bringing them to life! She has created city logos and enjoys sharing her artistic talents when needed. She is pursuing a career in zoology and wildlife management.

William, The What-If Wonder Book Series

The William, the What-If Wonder book series is designed to help children with anxiety learn how to navigate their worries when faced with the uncertainty of new situations. Every story focuses on a common childhood experience that may be overwhelming to a child with anxiety and begins to teach the child ways to manage that anxiety. William struggles with many anxious thoughts that dominate his day, but he uses different strategies such as problem solving and cognitive reframing to see these situations in a new way. These strategies remind him he has the power to find positive solutions to his perceived problems.

By following William's journey, children and families can learn useful strategies to conquer their own anxiety and take control over their anxious thoughts. A Note to Parents and Caregivers section, written by a board certified pediatric psychologist, is at the back of each book to further help children and families generalize these strategies to their own lives.

Book #1: *William, the What-If Wonder on His First Day of School*
Book #2: *William, the What-If Wonder and His Sleepover Worries*

CPSIA information can be obtained
at www.ICGtesting.com
Printed in the USA
BVRC091055200721
612310BV00016B/73